The Dragon of Almara

Her First Knight, Volume 4

Ash Gray

Published by Ash Gray, 2022.

THE DRAGON OF ALMARA

First edition. October 2, 2022.

Copyright © 2022 Ash Gray.

ISBN: 979-8224460724

Written by Ash Gray.

Chapter 1

Down in the snowy street, Luane, the Dragon of Almara, was an imposing figure, a giant brute of a woman standing beside her giant brute of a horse. Her blonde hair was wild and her blue eyes narrow and she wore silver armor, beautifully engraved, with the sigil of a roaring dragon on the breastplate. All of that was very hard to see in the blizzard, however, even though Luane was carrying a torch. Liadan and the others could see only a giant figure with yellow hair that was simply too large to be anyone else.

Liadan knew that some believed Rowan to be half giant, but Luane could have passed for a full giant, for she was taller even than the Black Lioness, standing at a staggering seven feet tall. The stories said she was half-Wildoras and half-giant, being so gargantuan in size and yet able to cast orange magick fire from her hands, fire that had consumed whole hamlets with its rage.

As far as Liadan was concerned, the stories were right. She wouldn't have been surprised if a woman of Wildoras had lain with a giant to create Luane, for it wasn't uncommon among the wild women, though it was frowned upon. Liadan's people used to speak of Luane with great disdain back in Wildoras. They would sit around their fires and tell stories of the Dragon, of how she brought shame to them by using her power to slay innocents, and how the youth of each tribe should view Luane as a tale of caution.

As a child, Liadan had listened in awe to the tales of Luane slaughtering entire villages for pay. She had been amazed by Luane's power and had even admired her ability to adapt to the world outside Wildoras. But now, as a grown woman who had to face Luane's fire, Liadan wasn't in awe. Liadan was about ready to wet her smallclothes.

Outside, the gusts of snow were building strength, but the cold did not seem to bother the Dragon, who peered with narrowed eyes up and down the street as she held her torch aloft. On Luane's back was a great two-handed sword, and the silver pommel gleamed watery in the guttering light of her torch when she turned.

"Shite. And of course, Saoirse only just left. She could have defended us easily," said Ethne.

"Perhaps," Liadan said grimly, "but I would rather Saoirse did not risk her life to defend us and place in jeopardy her wedding day. Rowan would never forgive us if Saoirse was slain. We would never forgive ourselves."

Ethne looked frustrated and on the verge of arguing. Instead, she gazed intently Liadan and said, "What do we do, Li? Flee out the back door?" with the sort of somber disposition that made Liadan think she might have thrown herself in the sea had Liadan but asked.

"Is she really so terrifying?" asked Ava in innocent wonder. She stared wide-eyed up at Liadan and Ethne, and gazing down at her, Liadan thought she did indeed look as doe-like as Rowan had often joked.

Ethne goggled at the princess. "She's a beast of a woman, even bigger than Rowan, for the sake of the gods, and you would ask—!"

"Liadan is the Knight of the Wild!" said Ava confidently. "No one can best her! Not even some giant knight with a giant sword!"

Liadan smiled to hear Ava's words. "While I am pleased by your confidence in me, my princess," she said gently, "there was a reason Saoirse wished to escort us to Hastow. There are very few who can best the Dragon. Not even a knight of the wild could."

Ava frowned. "But you're the greatest knight there ever was!"

Liadan looked down at Ava and wondered what she could have done to have deserved such doting. She had never actually fought in front of Ava against a worthy foe and had only slain men she had taken by surprise. True, she had slain many of Mairin's thugs while Ava watched in awe, but those ragged, underfed bounty hunters hadn't been much of a challenge. Even little Lysa, without training, had handled them well. And when slaying the assassins back at Caradin, Liadan had easily bested the poor women with magick. In truth, she had little to boast about.

And yet, for whatever reason, Ava believed Liadan far more skilled and powerful than she was in reality. Perhaps it was due to King Eyvor's fireside tales of Wildoras, of which Ava had been privy since she was a child. Whatever the case, the stories weren't true. Liadan was the best in her class, perhaps the best knight to graduate the academy in recent years, but she was not a *legend*. The Dragon of Almara was.

"The back door," agreed Liadan, looking at Ethne.

Ethne grimly nodded.

Ava gasped in disbelief when Liadan grabbed her by the arm, grabbed her saddle bags from the floor, and marched them from the room, pulling the princess along. Ethne grabbed Lysa's arm and did likewise, ignoring it when Lysa sputtered indignantly.

"I don't *believe* you!" Ava cried, golden hair flying out behind her as she staggered after Liadan. "You're supposed to be a fearless, honorable knight! An unconquerable woman of the wild!"

"I'd rather be alive and conquerable," panted Ethne behind Ava.

They left the corridor and stopped on the landing, where they peered over the rail. As usual, the tavern below was crowded. Women were drinking, laughing, and dancing, and the band was playing enthusiastically.

Liadan searched the crowd below and her heart skipped a beat: the Dragon of Almara was standing at the bar, ordering a pint from Grainne, who looked quite nervous. Luane went still, as if she sensed

Liadan watching her, and very slowly, she turned her head, and their eyes connected.

"Shite. She's seen us," muttered Ethne.

Smirking, Luane slowly lifted her gauntlet toward them and spread the silver fingers.

Liadan's eyes flew wide. "Get down!" she yelled and tackled Ava just in time: a ball of fire came rocketing toward them where they stood on the upstairs landing, shaking the walls and sending up shards of wood in a splash of fragments when it made impact with the railing.

Liadan could hear people screaming in the tavern below, could hear Ava, Ethne, and Lysa coughing. Through the smoke and fire, she saw Ethne and Lysa crouched against the wall opposite, coughing as Ethne tried to shield Lysa from the spreading flames.

Ava was likewise trembling and coughing as Liadan's arms clutched her tight. They were lying on their sides on the floor, as before them, Liadan's saddle bags were consumed by the flames.

"S-She cast fire from her hand!" coughed Ava in disbelief. "A huge fireball! Large enough to consume the building!"

"Now you know why they call her the Dragon," said Liadan darkly, but she went still when she heard boots on the stair: Luane was coming for them. And she was taking her time. *Thump. Thump. Thump.*

Ethne looked through the fire at Liadan, her gray eyes panicking. "We have to get out of here, Li!" she growled, lurching to her feet. "Now!" She helped Lysa stand, who was still coughing shrilly.

Liadan was helping Ava to her feet when Luane appeared at the top of the stair, towering in her silver armor, indifferent to the flames dancing around her. With her laughing eyes fixed on Liadan, she stepped slowly through the flames, her shadow falling over Ava, who shrank before her. Luane was lifting her hand again when Liadan bellowed, "NO!"

Liadan lunged protectively in front of Ava and felt the magick leapt out of her in an invisible blast, smacking with incredible force right in the center of Luane's breastplate. The giant woman was sent careening backward, straight through the wall, and into an unoccupied room, the walls of which crumbled around her in fragmented bricks and wood paneling. The force of the impact brought parts of the ceiling down, and as the Dragon was lurching beastlike to her feet, she was knocked down again by the sudden rain of debris.

Liadan waited breathlessly for Luane to burst out of the rubble, but she did not. Relief washed over her: they had time to get away.

"I *knew* you could stop her, my knight!" Ava cried, hugging Liadan's arm. She bounced up on tiptoe and pecked Liadan's cheek with her soft lips again and again, but Liadan was barely aware as all her attention was fixed on the rubble pile.

"Let us go! Stand not amazed!" growled Ethne, waving her hand in Liadan's face. "Before that monster rises again and slays us!"

"Liadan!" Lysa begged. Her face was smudged and she was frightened and coughing.

Liadan came back to reality, gazing from face to face. She had fallen into a trance of fear, waiting for Luane to rise. "You're right," she said hoarsely. "Let's go."

They mounted their horses and raced from Hargendon, flying fast through the white storm. As they galloped along at breakneck speed, Liadan held out her hand, and the blizzard parted before them like a curtain.

Liadan caught the others giving her curious looks and knew they were no doubt wondering why she hadn't used this power before. It was because she didn't have the power before. Knowing Ava and falling in love with her had awakened something in Liadan. Something she couldn't explain. But she was never so powerful as before the last few days.

Liadan led them south, pushing further and further from the cluster of villages behind them. Luane would eventually catch up to them, after all, and she did not wish for there to be casualties in the ensuing fight.

To their amazement, the winter storm, which had seemed to go on forever, suddenly began to clear. The wind dropped its screaming, falling abruptly silent, and the clouds overhead glided away, revealing a scattering of stars in the night sky. They pulled their horses to a stop at the height of an incline and remained still as the horses snorted mist in the sudden quiet.

Blank snow spread away from them to the bottom of a great valley, where ancient long barrows stood in rows either side, their stone doors surrounded by arched walls of brick and carved into the valley's sides.

"The Valley of Queens," whispered Ava, who was sitting the saddle before Liadan, snowflakes still sprinkled on the hood of her fur cloak. The hood was drawn up over her head, and Liadan could only see wisps of her golden hair. "The resting place of my ancestors," she said, awe-stricken and hushed.

Each realm in the seven kingdoms had two ancient valleys, one for the kings and one for the queens. The valley they had come to, with them being in Illa, belonged to House Damaris. Liadan could see the great statue of the goddess Eyslath in the distance. She stood at the other end of the valley, towering over the dead queens, her six arms spread and her sleeves hanging from them like water.

"But how do you know it's the Valley of Queens?" wondered Ethne, who was sitting astride her white stallion behind Lysa. She nodded at the valley below. "Those could be kings down there."

"I can feel it in my bones," Ava whispered in a trembling voice and said no more.

Liadan knew what was going through Ava's mind. If not for the Endoreth invasion and the alliance with Almara, Ava would have remained at Caradin. She would have become queen, ruled the realm for decades, and eventually gone to her eternal rest in the valley of her kin. Now perhaps she would die senselessly, slaughtered by Luane's magick or by random bandits in the woods, and her grave would be shallow and unmarked.

Somehow, Liadan knew Ava was wishing she was as clever as her father had supposed, she knew the princess was wishing she had orchestrated a coup and taken the crown from her father. The princess could have then gathered allies on her own and led her people against King Bjorn and Endoreth's armies. It wouldn't have been easy, but it would have been better than selling herself in a marriage.

But because Ava was not witty or pragmatic or even ruthless, she was here, living on the run, her life in constant peril, sleeping in the snow and the mud, wearing the same gown every day. Because she was meek and spoiled and useless, she was here. Liadan could feel the bitterness and sorrow welling up in Ava as the princess gazed almost longingly across the Valley of Queens.

Liadan didn't know why, but she had been able to read Ava's mind a great deal lately. Back at the tavern in Hargendon, for instance, she had felt Ava's rage-fueled desire to cut off the head of the man who groped her, and Liadan had obeyed to please her. Even when she was furious at Ava… Liadan always found herself trying to please her.

"It feels almost eerie here," Lysa said, hugging her cloak to her throat and shivering. She looked very tired and unhappy, her brown hair tousled under her hood, her eyes lined. She was still wearing her leather armor and sword beneath her cloak. "But at least the storm has lifted," she said with relief.

"It hasn't," said Ethne, gazing back over her shoulder.

Liadan looked over her shoulder as well: the storm was raging on behind them. The sheets of snow and icy wind howled just beyond the edge of the valley, as if there was some invisible barrier the storm could not pass. Liadan, having grown up in Wildoras, had seen such magick before, but only in the wilds. She wondered what wild woman magi House Damaris had employed to cast such a spell over the valley.

"A magick barrier. Let us take advantage of it," said Liadan, taking up the reins of her brown horse again. She nodded at the valley below. "Let us hide ourselves in one of these tombs before Luane has found us here gawping."

Ava gasped. "We can't disturb the tombs! They're my ancestors and the goddess Eyslath will—"

"I'm sure your ancestors wouldn't want you to die at the hands of the Dragon, your highness," said Ethne. She also took up the reins of her stallion, reaching around Lysa. She nodded grimly at Liadan. "Let us venture in."

House Damaris was one of the oldest houses in the seven kingdoms, going back to the age of the elves, when the elven had ruled the land alongside humans, before their sudden and mysterious disappearance. As a result, there were thousands of tombs, one beside the other, like little doors under the hill, and the valley seemed to go on forever, rising above them on both sides.

The only sound was the faint jingle of the knights' armor and the crunch of horse hooves over the snow. The magick barrier appeared to keep most of the snow out, and as a result, the snow wasn't very deep at all and fell only in a thin layer. Liadan was grateful for that, as they would not have been able to reach any of the tombs to hide themselves. The snow was also so thin that they didn't leave an obvious trail for Luane to follow. Instead, the horses clomped softly through a fine sprinkling of snow from which patches of mud and grass could be seen. They made good time down the valley as a result.

"We should choose one quickly if we are to do this," said Lysa in a low voice when they had already passed six tombs, "though shutting ourselves in a tomb with little air seems foolish."

Liadan glanced at Lysa irritably. Lysa was always complaining but never had any ideas of her own. Liadan didn't know how Ethne could stand her or what she saw in the tiny handmaiden beyond her admittedly ripe breasts and tight—

"The tombs have passages leading out of the valley," said Ava quietly. "They are not without air."

Lysa and Ethne looked around at Ava in surprise, and Liadan didn't blame them: it hadn't occurred to any of them that Ava actually *knew* things about the world. Not only had the princess been shut away for her entire life, but according to Lysa, Ava hadn't much interest in learning and had only read books to escape into fantasy.

Ava blushed miserably as everyone stared at her and she admitted, "The romance series . . . *Knights of Illa, Part XXVI* . . . In that story, the knights hide in the tombs of House Damaris with the princess. They both have s-sex with her in the tomb," (Ava blushed brighter) "and the goddess Eyslath is angered by their defilement of the tomb and curses them, so they are forced to flee the valley through a back tunnel . . ."

"So as long as we don't have group sex on the queen's sarcophagus, Eyslath won't try to kill us," said Ethne, her lips pulling in a crooked smile as she gazed down the valley at the enormous statue.

Lysa made an impatient noise. "Those are just romance novels, your highness," she said in exasperation.

Ava frowned, annoyed now. "Beathan Macclellan didn't just write romance novels! She was a historian and all of her books were accurate!"

Ethne raised her brows, her head bobbing as the white horse carried her along. "Hmm. Learn something new every day. I always thought Macclellan was trash, myself."

Ava glared sideways at Ethne. Then something occurred to her and she smiled as she teased, "*You* read romance novels?"

"In my youth," said Ethne, grinning.

"Do you remember which tomb they hid in, my princess?" Liadan asked. "Perhaps that tomb alone has an escape tunnel, while the others do not."

"Good thinking," said Ethne.

"It was the tomb of Queen Saraid," said Ava thoughtfully.

"Ah," said Ethne, blinking. "The warrior queen." She frowned. "I wonder why Saraid would have an escape tunnel in the back of her tomb.

I mean, she was dead. If the tomb was flooded or some other, why would she need to escape?"

"They say that she faked her own death," Ava answered, amused, "and that she escaped out of the tunnel and ran away with the elves. Saraid supposedly had an elven lover who took Saraid with her to . . . wherever the elves went."

"So if we enter the tomb," Ethne realized, "Saraid's coffin will be empty?"

"If the legends are true," Ava answered. "Some believe the legend only exists to explain away the absence of the corpse. In reality, Saraid's tomb was raided, but the thief couldn't get her out of her armor, so he took the whole corpse."

"Disgusting!" cried Lysa while Ethne howled with laughter.

"Do you believe any of this horse shite, Liadan?" laughed Ethne.

Liadan was hardly paying attention to the others. Her eyes were scanning each tomb door they passed, looking for the symbols and signifiers that would mark the occupier. Queen Saraid's symbol had been the rune symbol Fehu, which Liadan had always thought looked like a tree with only two branches on one side. The rune would be enclosed by a triangle, with many "heatwave" lines coming from it. Liadan knew because she had been forced to study the runes of the entire Damaris dynasty at the academy . . . which had been no riveting feat.

Ava, however, noticed the tomb of Saraid before Liadan did. "There it is," Ava said, voice yet again hushed and awed.

Liadan and Ethne pulled their horses to a stop.

Ava was right: the tomb of Queen Saraid was on their immediate left, overrun with dead vines and flowers and muddy grass, all of which peeped brown and lifeless from beneath a thin layer of snow. Liadan could see the arched brick wall, crumbling with the slow passage of time, and in the center of the bricks, the stone door, also covered in a web of dead brown vines. It looked as if no one had been there for centuries.

Liadan dismounted, her eyes on the tomb. She had the strange feeling that entering the place was about to change her world forever. She couldn't shake it. Her, the knight who was exiled and forbidden to rule, would become a ruler if she set foot in that tomb. The whispers of it echoed in her mind. Where did the whispers come from? She wondered if the others were hearing whispers, but when she glanced around, none of them seemed bothered.

"How do we open the door?" wondered Ethne, also dismounting. "Even you can't open it, Li. The way I understand it, these doors were immensely heavy to keep out thieves, and it took the help of giants to place them in the first place! Back when giants weren't trying to rape us and eat us, that is."

Ethne reached up and lifted Lysa down from the horse, setting her on her feet. Lysa looked intrigued by what Ethne had said, and Liadan was beginning to notice that Lysa only seemed to take stories seriously when they were coming from Ethne. She almost always dismissed Ava. Perhaps it was Ethne's old bard charm shining through. The Knight of the Sparrow could charm anyone into caring about her tales.

"Really?" said Lysa, gazing up at Ethne eagerly. "The giants were our friends once?"

"Oh yes," said Ethne, gazing around the valley as if it impressed her. "It would have been fascinating to have examined these tombs under different circumstances."

"These are my ancestors, lest you forget!" said Ava hotly. "Their tombs should remain intact and unbefouled!" She was still sitting on Liadan's horse and folded her arms, indignant.

"Oh—of course, your highness," said Ethne, playfully bowing.

Ava rolled her eyes. Then she held out her arms and lifted her chin. "Lift me down, my knight!"

Liadan obeyed, reaching up and taking Ava by her narrow waist. She set the princess gently on her feet. Then Liadan turned and – with the others watching in confusion – she lifted her hand and focused, sending all of her magick, all of its strength, to the heavy stone door of the tomb. Sweat beaded on her brow as she silently strained with effort. She saw the heavy stone door move slightly and frowned, focusing harder, and in seconds, the round, flat stone door had rolled aside, revealing a dark passage. Liadan lowered her hand and heard the others gasping.

"How did you do that?" cried Ava with a sort of happy ecstasy and took Liadan's arm, peering up at her.

"I don't know," Liadan answered breathlessly. She had never before been able to move things with her mind, but back at Hargendon, she had moved Luane, and now, she had opened a tomb. It had to be Ava. Nothing else made sense.

There had been stories back in Wildoras that once a wild woman found a compatible mate, then she would become what she was truly meant to be, growing in power and might. Liadan's power had been strengthening since she'd met Ava, to the point that she had been able to defend the princess from would-be assassins with ease and on her own back at Caradin. Now she could move things with her mind, and she felt an overwhelming desire to impregnate Ava . . . To rip off Ava's clothes and finger her, until the seed had passed through her fingertips and into Ava's sex . . . Until her woman produced a child as mighty as her parent . . . In essence, Ava had triggered the mating urge in Liadan.

Liadan didn't quite know what to do. This was a bad time to procreate, out here in the middle of nowhere, while living on the run. But she also felt that if she didn't, she would combust.

"You're amazing!" Ava cried breathlessly.

When Liadan looked down, Ava was gazing up at her, her pretty green eyes wide in wonder and admiration, her cleavage heaving, so soft and plump. The princess looked so sweet, innocent, and beautiful, her face framed beneath her hood by wisps of golden hair. Liadan wanted to rip her clothes off. The urge swept over her – more powerful than it had ever been – but she held it down and turned away. Her clitoris, however, was raging in her smallclothes.

"Come," said Ethne, leading the horses forward. She appeared calm, though Liadan could tell she was as shocked as everyone else by Liadan's new abilities. Ethne passed Ava the reins of Liadan's brown horse as she said, "Lead us inside and hurry! We linger here as if a dangerous magi weren't on our trail!"

"She's right," said Lysa, though she was still gazing at Liadan with something between amazement and caution.

Liadan turned away, and lifting her hand, she conjured a golden wisp to it, the ball of hovering light casting their faces in shadow as they all entered the tomb. But the horses, not at all pleased by the prospect of going underground, bucked and nickered, kicking their legs wildly. Liadan's horse nearly kicked Ava, who managed to dodge narrowly when Liadan grabbed Ava around the waist and pulled her back.

Ethne struggled with her horse for a while, then gave up and unbuckled her saddle bags. She smacked the white horse's bottom, and it took off into the valley again. Liadan did likewise with her own horse, and the group watched for a moment as the horses tore away, galloping so fast it was as if the Dragon herself were casting flames behind them.

- "Now we have no horses," said Lysa crossly.

"I dunno," said Ethne, shifting the saddle bags onto her shoulder. "We could always ride you."

"Very funny," said Lysa sarcastically.

Liadan stepped forward and rolled the stone door back into place with her mind, closing them in such darkness that it was hard to see each other, even with the magick of Liadan's golden wisp light. Then, preparing to head down the tunnel, she took Ava's hand, and something hot jumped through their fingers. Ava didn't seem to notice the heat, but Liadan quickly took her hand away: her fingertips were glowing. They were glowing a bright gold, and she could see her fingerprints and veins, as if her fingertips had turned transparent from the light.

"What is it?" asked Ava innocently. She seemed unfazed by Liadan's glowing fingers, and it was because Liadan's fingers often glowed when she cast magick.

But Liadan knew her fingers were glowing for a different reason entirely. By touching Ava's skin, Liadan's body had reacted to Ava and had started the process. If Liadan were to finger Ava again, she would impregnate the princess.

Chapter 2

Ava sensed something strange was happening with Liadan, but knowing that the grim and stoic knight would eventually come around in her own time, Ava decided to say nothing of it, instead turning her attention to the fascinating tomb they had only just entered. There were colorful paintings on the walls, though most of them showed mundane, everyday events: Queen Saraid brushing her long yellow hair, Queen Saraid waving to crowds during a parade, Queen Saraid drinking wine on a pleasure barge with her lover, a burly female knight known as Brianag the Black. It wasn't until they had been walking down the tunnel for some time that Ava noticed a panel that was actually interesting.

"Look!" Ava cried in excitement and halted in her tracks.

Liadan and the others halted as well and followed Ava's gaze: the hieroglyphs and paintings behind Liadan's head told the story of Queen Saraid's greatest battle, the Battle of Black Tears . . .. which she'd fought against Endoreth during an invasion of Illa. The battle had been referred to for centuries as "the Black Tears incident" because Queen Saraid had used the fire of a dragon to decimate King Azmon's armies. She was successful, but only for so long. King Azmon was long-lived due to an ancient spell that had been lost to women long before, and once Queen Saraid, the protector of the seven realms, and her great dragon were dead and gone, King Azmon made his move, invading the seven realms and finally conquering them, securing the rulership of men. And just like that, because a man had learned to use magick, the age of woman had ended.

Ava stared up at the image of Queen Saraid, who stood powerful in her golden battle armor, her golden hair streaming in the wind, her sword lifted, and she thought her ancestor would be ashamed of her. Instead of fighting for her realm, Ava was running. Instead of caring for her people, Ava was leaving them behind to be invaded and ruled by King Bjorn! She was a spoiled, lazy princess who didn't even know how to wield politics as a weapon, let alone a sword. Queen Saraid would have despised her.

As if she sensed what was going through Ava's mind, Liadan frowned sadly and placed a comforting hand on Ava's shoulder. Liadan had been guessing Ava's thoughts and feelings quite accurately lately, and a part of her hated it. She was weak and pathetic and Liadan pitied her. How she hated that Liadan knew of her internal struggle, and yet, how she marveled that Liadan knew. Something powerful was brewing between them, though Ava could not understand what.

"But what does it mean?" wondered Lysa bitterly, for she had never really learned all of her runes. In fact, she was the only one in their group who was undereducated, which was why Ava wasn't angry with Lysa for dismissing her earlier: Lysa had only dismissed Ava's romance novels because she was jealous that she herself couldn't fully read.

"It's a story," Ava answered, "of how Queen Saraid fought back Endoreth during King Azmon's invasion . . . It's a sign from the goddess that my running is cowardly. Queen Saraid would disown me to see what selfish thing I have done."

"Don't say that," said Liadan, frowning. "There is nothing wrong with living for yourself and not wishing to rule—"

"I have a duty, an *obligation* to my people! If I won't defend them, who will?" Ava said over Liadan, more loudly than she intended. "My father? He can't even find his dick to make new heirs!" Catching her breath – and shocked by her own angry words—Ava marched on, not looking back to see if the others followed.

When they came at last to the chamber where Queen Saraid's coffin stood, the room was much larger than Ava could have anticipated, even from having read about it in her romance novels. It was a circular room, with golden floors and walls, still glittering from having been air-sealed for thousands of years. Queen Saraid's golden coffin stood in the center of the room on a dais, and all around it lay offerings and gifts: piles of gold, displayed weapons, golden bowls of sparkling jewels, and stands with the dead queen's beautifully engraved golden armor.

At the foot of the queen's coffin were two more coffins, gold but not as grand as Queen Saraid's. One Ava recognized as belonging to Brianag the Black, for the knight's house sigil – the crow – was upon it. The second coffin was much smaller than the other two, as if a shorter person lay inside, and after reading the runes on the lid, Ava knew it belonged to Saraid's handmaiden . . . and most trusted friend.

Ava looked around at Lysa, who was standing nearby with Ethne, looking pale and frightened as she glanced around the chamber. If Ava had been queen, Lysa would have been buried with her in a grand tomb like this, surrounded by piles of gold and gifts, with paintings on the walls depicting what their everyday lives had been like.

On the other side of the chamber, just as Ava had predicted, there was a tunnel leading to another exit. Ava found that pleasing but also curious. Why would an exit tunnel have been placed in a tomb? She was half-tempted to open Saraid's coffin and see if the queen was really inside.

"We've been riding for hours," said Ethne, tiredly dropping her saddle bags to the floor. "What do you say we rest here for a while, Li? Then we can pick up and keep going toward Hastow."

"Not toward Hastow," said Liadan sternly. "Luane would just follow us, and then the people there would come to danger. Her magick is chaotic and she cares not for how many innocents are slain as she passes."

"Where then shall we go?" said Lysa, impatiently folding her arms. "Shall we just wander the wilderness, waiting for Luane to catch up with us?"

Ava noticed Liadan tighten with irritation. The Knight of the Wild whirled and said in a level voice, "Let us pretend that Lysa is in charge. Let us pretend for one day and one night. All that we do and wherever we shall go is henceforth in Lysa's hands." She stared down at Lysa for a long time, and Lysa slowly turned pink.

Ethne scowled and placed a protective arm around Lysa. "Liadan! What the hell's the matter with you?"

Determined not to be bothered, Lysa lifted her chin and casually shrugged Ethne's arm off. "I shall hold you to your word then, knight," she said haughtily to Liadan. "We shall stay here for two hour's rest. Liadan, you shall open the door at the end of the escape tunnel to let in some air. Then you shall take first watch as the rest of us take our rest—"

"And afterwards?" prompted Liadan, who seemed amused by Lysa's haughty confidence.

Lysa hesitated. "A-Afterward we will continue south, to the river."

Ava had been studying the hieroglyphs and paintings on the chamber walls, but she turned to face Lysa, intrigued. "You mean to approach Godga. The river witch," she said. It wasn't a question.

Lysa smiled.

Ava was more than intrigued now. Back when Lysa had first encouraged her to run away, she had thought often of running far south, past the eastern wood, to the river, where old Godga guarded the bridge to Wildoras. The river was enchanted and could not be crossed through any normal means. Only the women of Wildoras could cross without trouble. Others had to make an exchange with the witch. Not many had attempted it, for not only was the price often quite steep, but the women of Wildoras were not welcoming of outsiders and were so terrifying in their magick might that even a bounty hunter or a greedy mercenary like Luane would never dare venture in.

Ava knew that even if they couldn't barter passage, they could always lie there in wait at the bridge, allow Luane to approach and trick her into a battle with the Magi Godga. Godga was one of the most powerful magi in the seven realms: the Dragon of Almara would not stand a chance. Ava knew this was Lysa's intention, and they traded smiles.

"Godga?" said Ethne, her face twisting. "The river hag? She's dangerous! Liadan, you can't allow this!" She looked to Liadan in amazement.

Ava looked to Liadan as well, but far from being concerned or afraid, the Knight of the Wild seemed to approve of Lysa's plan. She was staring down at Lysa and smiling steadily. "It shall be as you say, *little Lysa*," she said . . . with a husky sort of flirtatiousness that made Lysa color up.

And indeed, remembering the night Liadan had made love to them both, Ava held down a blush.

With their plans laid out, they set about getting ready to rest. Ethne rolled out the bedroll she would share with Lysa, and Ava could hear the two of them bickering back and forth about the Godga. Ethne didn't trust what she referred to as "wild magi" (the hypocrisy, Ava thought, since Ethne was friends with a magi) while Lysa insisted that the Godga was their only chance of survival, the risk of it be damned. Even after they were snuggling in the bedroll together, they continued their argument, their voices growing softer as they fell asleep against each other.

Ava was exhausted and wanted to roll out Liadan's bedroll for herself, but she also wanted to continue studying the hieroglyphs in the chamber. They would be leaving very soon, and she wanted to see and memorize as much of it as she could. It was one thing to learn about Queen Saraid in a history lesson. It was another thing entirely to actually see her tomb and ancient depictions of her life!

A few minutes had passed when Ava heard Liadan return from having opened the door at the end of the back tunnel. The knight's armor jingled softly and her boots thumped as she drew near Ava. The smell of steel, leather, and musky sweat preceded her, as it always did.

"You shall not believe what I have seen at the end of the back tunnel," Liadan said breathlessly.

Ava glanced over her shoulder at Liadan and halted in surprise: the Knight of the Wild looked as if she had seen a ghost. She was pale and breathless, pink-cheeked, and her red hair was tousled as if she'd run. She gulped for air as Ava stared at her in concern. To Ava's relief, Liadan smiled.

"Worry not," Liadan said. "It is nothing frightening or terrible. I think my princess shall be quite intrigued, in fact."

"So you found more hieroglyphs?" asked Ava, feeling the excitement bubbling.

Liadan only smiled again. "This is better than hieroglyphs. I think you shall be quite amazed."

Frustrated, Ava turned away and examined the images on the walls again. "You are cruel to withhold it, whatever it is," she said with a laugh.

"Cruel, my princess? No. Rather, I enjoy seeing you beg," said Liadan behind her.

Ava laughed again, blushing a little as the meaning behind Liadan's words slowly occurred to her. She felt Liadan's large hand squeeze her shoulder and knew without turning that the knight was aroused. She was correct: Liadan breathed hard and massaged Ava's shoulder, and her hand was slightly trembling with the need. She pushed aside Ava's long golden hair and kissed her neck.

Ava moaned and bit her lip. "Here? Now?"

"My princess . . ." Liadan whispered. "The sight of your sweet face and your great breasts . . . it is driving me wild. Wilder than I ever . . ."

Ava's heart fluttered, delighted by Liadan's hungry words. She looked over her shoulder and went still in surprise to see how Liadan's blue eyes suffered as they gazed down at her. "What is it?" she cried in alarm.

"Shh," Liadan begged, glancing anxiously toward the place where Ethne and Lysa slept in their bedroll. She glanced down and miserably held out her hands, so that they were before Ava.

Ava looked down. Liadan's fingertips were glowing – all ten of them. Liadan had removed her gauntlets and was holding her fingers spread so that Ava could see. The light was glowing from within, making Liadan's fingerprints and veins stand out and giving her skin the illusion of being transparent. Ava hesitated and cupped Liadan's hands in her own. She gasped. They were pleasantly hot, and when she closed her fingers over them, a delicious tingle went through her. She felt her sex swell and blushed bright.

"What's h-happening?" Ava stammered, breathless and flushed with arousal. "It feels amazing!"

Liadan laughed sadly. "When a woman of Wildoras finds a compatible mate," she explained, "her body . . . begins the breeding process."

Ava quickly looked up and nearly laughed: Liadan was blushing faintly and looked agonizingly embarrassed.

"My body is reacting to you," Liadan answered. "It is a bit akin to when a man has stiffened yet finds no release. My fingers glow, wanting to release my seed inside you, but to do so now, in the middle of all this chaos . . ."

Ava tried yet again not to laugh: Liadan was trapped in perpetual arousal. . . . because she loved Ava.

"Are you saying your body wants you to . . . impregnate me?" Ava asked in wonder. "And it will happen through your fingertips?"

"That is how it is done," Liadan admitted heavily. "I have only told you so that you shall understand why I must . . . refrain from touching you. I didn't mean to kiss you just now, but you were standing there, so soft and beautiful . . . And I . . . Ava!" Liadan gasped, for Ava had taken Liadan's hand and placed it over her sex, on top of her skirts.

"Ava," Liadan begged in a whisper. "We mustn't! If you were to become with child—"

"Make love to me, Liadan," Ava commanded, regally lifting her chin and crushing her soft golden hair under Liadan's nose. She knew the sweet, flowery smell would drive the knight wild, and she was correct: in a sudden frenzy, Liadan ripped open Ava's gown. Ava's back arched and she gasped as her great breasts trembled free, and as Liadan cupped one of her breasts and groped it hard, she yanked up Ava's skirt and crammed her other hand down the front of Ava's panties.

Ava arched her back against Liadan, frowning through the pleasure as she was fingered hard and groped, as the knight buried frantic kisses on her neck and the naked flesh of her shoulder. In a daze of pleasure, she reached back and cupped Liadan's face with one small hand. Liadan continued fingering Ava – so aggressively that Ava's hips were jerking in rhythm and her breasts were trembling. There was a moment when the Knight of the Wild gazed down at her, watched her breasts tremble and her cheeks blush with narrowed blue eyes, then she kissed Ava roughly on the mouth, thrusting her tongue against Ava's in a passionate kiss.

Ava could feel the moisture sliding down her thighs, and as Liadan made savage love to her, she moaned through their kiss and trembled, climaxing with a helpless, muffled cry.

AVA DIDN'T UNDERSTAND why Liadan was so afraid of impregnating her. Ava had already decided that she meant to return to Caradin and rule Illa, and if she already had a daughter as her heir, all the better. In the time of the elves, before the curse of the gods was placed on Wildoras, it was the women who had ruled each of the seven realms, and they were not known as "kingdoms" then, for there had been no kings. It wasn't until after the fall of Wildoras (and the fall of women) that the first king was crowned – King Azmon of Realm Hallivere, often hailed as the first and only male magi to have ever existed.

Queen Saraid had lived during the ancient times, when women had ruled the land and only their daughters were their heirs. Seeing the hieroglyphics in the dead queen's tomb had lit in a fire in Ava. After the way her father had treated her – joking about her being forced to lay with Prince Cassian!—after all she had suffered for the sake of an arranged marriage, and after the destruction caused by King Bjorn's ridiculous conquest, she knew now that the gods had made a mistake in casting down women and uplifting men. Lysa was right: men caused nothing but destruction and suffering for others. They were no more fit to rule than small, temperamental children as far as she was concerned. But she was no longer going to flee from it. She was going to do something about it.

Ava knew it would have been easier if she, like Queen Saraid, had access to trained dragons. But all the most powerful dragons were dead and gone. The dragons that existed today were small, couldn't even speak, and were devolved, base, animal-like creatures who knew only breeding and mating. Attempting to tame one was suicide, but because these wild dragons were still a danger to the world at large, entire academies of knights had been trained to hunt and slay them. Dragon blood, teeth, and scales were also quite rare and expensive, and so, just slaying one dragon could make the poorest knight quite wealthy. Rowan hadn't been wrong about that much.

After taking turns resting in the ancient tomb, Ava, Liadan, Ethne, and Lysa packed up their bedrolls and set out yet again, walking down the exit tunnel, guided by the golden wisp that hovered over Liadan's shoulder. Ava stared often at the wisp, thinking she would have many strong daughters brimming with magic might, who would rule this land and take it back for women. No longer would women be bartered and exchanged like chattel in arranged marriages! No longer would women be the possessions of their fathers and husbands! A new day was dawning, and it was dawning in Ava's womb.

Though Liadan's seed had filled her only hours before, Ava's womb had been burning hot ever since, as if something were roasting away inside her. She couldn't fathom what was happening, but she had to suppose it was the result of a magickal pregnancy. She had not, after all, become pregnant by normal means. She had become pregnant by a woman, through some sort of spell Liadan's fingers had cast, and now she could feel something growing rapidly inside her. Perhaps several somethings.

They had been walking for what felt like half an hour when the escape tunnel suddenly opened upon another cavern. This cavern was sheeted in gold as Queen Saraid's had been, but there was water damage, and roots were dangling from the ceiling in a spidery web. If not for Liadan's golden light, it would have been completely dark. At the far side of the cavern, moonlight spilled cold through an open doorway, the stone door of which had been rolled aside by Liadan to let in air, but there was something there, in the center of the cavern, something the moonlight only barely touched.

"This way," said Liadan, who sounded in awe. "We shall have to walk around it."

"Walk around what?" said Lysa somewhere behind Ava.

Ava saw Liadan smile. Then the barbarian knight gestured at the hovering wisplight, causing it to expand and grow brighter. As the golden light spread slowly, filling the dark room, Ava gasped at what she saw: there, enormous as a mountain, grinned the ancient skull of a dragon.

"Goddess!" Lysa gasped, pointing. "Ava, look! A dragon egg!"

Ava looked where Lysa had pointed, and sure enough, there was a dragon egg beside the great dragon skull. It was displayed neatly in a golden bowl on a low table, glittering and green. The egg was about the size of a newborn baby. It lay on a pile of gold coins like a jewel.

"Gods be good!" swore Ethne, drawing near.

Ava looked up at Liadan in amazement.

"I told you it would intrigue thee," said Liadan, pleased.

"You should take it," said Ethne.

Ava scowled. "If you think I'm going to sell it –! Not that it wouldn't bring in a great deal of coin," she admitted grudgingly.

"Sell it? No, no," said Ethne, waving a hand. "They say a dragon egg can stay dormant for a thousand years! And if you put it in the fire, it will still hatch! You should take it so you can *hatch* it and raise it up!"

Ava felt her heart quickening at the thought. Her eyes grew almost feverish as she stared down at the egg on its pile of gold.

"Ethne has a point," said Lysa, who was hushed and amazed as she stared at the egg. "You were going on about taking back Illa for your bloodline. A dragon is the surest way. It's not like you have an army."

Ava leaned down, and very carefully, she wrapped the egg in her fur cloak, as if she was bundling a baby in her arms. When she stood again, she felt heat in her cheeks and arms, and she realized it was radiating from the egg. Hold it was like sitting near a blazing fire. It was . . .wonderful.

"It feels alive," Ava said in amazement. "There's a living dragon in here!"

"We should take the gold in that bowl, too," said Ethne thoughtfully.

Ava glared at the Sparrow Knight.

Ethne shrugged. "Look . . . We don't know how much longer we're going to be on the road," she said. "We may need that coin for a tavern. Unless you *like* sleeping in the mud and snow," she added pointedly.

"Fine," said Ava grudgingly and gestured at the ornate bowl.

Lysa stepped forward and helped Ethne empty the pile of gold coins into her saddle bags. It looked like just enough coins for several stays at a tavern, and if she had to admit it, Ava was pleased, for she did indeed despise sleeping in the cold and filth.

Ava looked around and noticed Liadan was frowning. "What is it, my knight?" the princess asked.

Liadan hesitated. "It's just that . . . A dragon wouldn't be allowed in Wildoras. My people despise them, for they are destructive and wild, wreaking havoc on our camps and eating our livestock. We shall have to find some other place to hide until the time when we can take back Illa, my princess."

Ava frowned. She hadn't known that. She gazed apologetically at Liadan, knowing that the knight had been looking forward to seeing her homeland again, but Liadan gave Ava a reassuring smile.

"I told you about the egg because I want you to succeed. I could have easily hidden its existence," said Liadan. "My duty is to love you and aid you. If it means I cannot return to Wildoras, then so be it. Helping you retake Illa is more important. Your happiness is more important."

Ava wanted to protest, but Liadan turned away, gesturing for her hovering light-wisp to follow her.

"Let us move along then," said the Knight of the Wild. From the corner of her eye, she was watching Ava and seemed pleased that she was pleased: Ava could not stop smiling. And why should she? By stumbling across this egg in her ancestor's tomb, she had discovered the key to retaking her throne.

Chapter 3

Outside, the eastern wood greeted them, its trees standing naked of leaves in the cold. They were beyond the valley now, for the blizzard had descended fast upon them, and they then spent the night walking against it, looking for shelter from the cold. Eventually, they noticed what they assumed to be bloody animal tracks in the snow and followed them to a cave, hoping to find easy game. To their horror, there was a man inside the cave entrance . . . and both his arms were gone.

Ethne observed that the man was a peasant, perhaps a farmer from Wedale, for he had the look of the corn people about him. He lay there panting and weeping, draped in filthy rags. His hair was matted, and the stumps of his arms were bleeding profusely, as if his arms had only just been removed. He lay on the floor of the cave, writhing in agony. Liadan announced that he was sick with disease, and knowing there was nothing they could do for him, she pulled a knife from her boot, intending to slit the man's throat. Everyone else retreated outside as the deed the done.

Even after the man was put out of his misery and taken out to be buried by the quick-falling snow, no one wanted to remain in the cave. There were trails of blood near the entrance, from the man having dragged himself after falling on his face, and the stink of his sickness was still on the air. But the blizzard was raging hard, and they had nowhere else to take shelter, and so, against their own inclinations, they set up camp there in the cave and ate bread and dried meat while sitting around the fire that Liadan conjured with her magick.

Ava had taken her torn nightgown and fashioned it into a makeshift sling. She wrapped the sling around her chest and let the dragon egg rest inside it, almost as if it were a babe at its mother's breasts. She hadn't let the egg out of her sight since taking it from the tomb and seemed intent on keeping it near. Ethne wanted to have a look at it but knew better than to ask. Ava wouldn't even let anyone hold the egg.

They ate in silence as the fire crackled and leapt, but Ethne knew everyone was thinking about the armless man. How could they not? Such a bizarre thing to have happened! But everyone was afraid to talk about it! Ethne was tired of being afraid and decided to break the silence.

"That man," Ethne said thoughtfully, chewing on her bread.

Liadan went still and looked quickly at Ethne. Lysa had been in the act of drinking water from a skin and paused. Ava chewed miserably on her dried meat and didn't raise her eyes.

"I mean, how did he lose his arms?" Ethne wondered. "Even wolves wouldn't brave this blizzard for a snack, and the wounds looked clean-cut, not ragged from teeth. Poor bastard."

"He came from the south," Lysa said. "His tracks were outside, remember? Bloody tracks in the snow. It's how we found the cave in the first place."

"Yes, but we thought it was a wounded animal," said Ethne. "So strange. I wonder if he was a shapeshifter. Maybe he turned into a fox and got caught in a trap." She laughed at the thought. "But that's not possible, is it?" She looked from face to face. "Men cannot wield magick."

"There was one," said Ava darkly, and Ethne knew the princess was referring to King Azmon, who had used magick to overthrow women and remove them from power across the seven realms.

"Yes, but Azmon has been dead a thousand years now," said Ethne.

"Obviously, someone else removed his arms," said Lysa. "He was filthy and looked as if he hadn't eaten in days. He was someone's prisoner. And for whatever reason, they cut off his arms and abandoned him here."

"But there were no other tracks in the snow," Ethne pointed out. "And he couldn't have crawled all the way here in the blizzard. Not bleeding like that. Just gets stranger and stranger, doesn't it?"

"He was sent here by magick," said Liadan in a low voice.

Everyone looked at her.

"Before I killed him," Liadan went on somberly, "he told me he was a defector from King Eyvor's army. He tried to cross the Breandan Bridge and head south into the wilds. Old Godga set the toll as a riddle. He failed and had to pay with his arms. . . . He thought she'd meant his armor and weapons. She took those as well."

"Damn," said Ethne, shaking her head. "That is beyond cruel! Are we sure we want to keep going south?"

"Where else can we hide from Luane if not behind Godga?" said Liadan, shrugging. "We could turn about and make for Hastow, but it's too far away now. Luane would find us first."

Ethne didn't feel comforted by Liadan's words. Somehow, she knew they would all regret going to Godga. Ethne wondered unhappily if things weren't about to become very sinister.

"Is the war so terrible that men are defecting?" asked Ava, gazing intently at Liadan.

Liadan grimly nodded. "Bjorn's armies are decimating Eyvor's. It's brutal. I expect there'll be more deserters in these parts soon. All the more reason to keep moving. Men are dangerous, especially men who have seen war."

"That armless man didn't look so dangerous," said Lysa with a snort. "In fact, I'd say it was the magi who were the dangerous ones."

Liadan went still.

Ava slowly looked up in amazement. "How can you say that, Lysa? After all your speeches about the evils of men? And after all the times Liadan hath protected thee!"

"Oh, I know men are dangerous," Lysa answered – with a bitterness that surprised Ethne. "That doesn't make magi less so. I hope Luane and Godga destroy each other." Lysa glared at the fire and said no more.

"And I hope Bjorn and my father destroy each other," Ava said, shocking Ethne with her sudden malice. Though Ethne noticed that Liadan, rather than being shocked, only looked sorry for Ava.

Ava thoughtfully returned to her dry meat, and Ethne knew she was likely thinking of her father. Given the might of Bjorn's armies – and without an alliance from Almara – it was only a matter of time before the capital fell and King Eyvor was either taken prisoner or executed. Ava was angry with her father for disowning her, but the princess was not entirely certain she wanted the man executed, that much Ethne knew. No, despite her bitter words, Ava was too gentle for all of that. Even her plan for taking her rightful throne, angry as she was, had likely never involved hurting her father.

Ava finished her bread and dried meat and went to bed, curling up in Liadan's bedroll and looking a little grim and sad as she hugged her dragon egg. Lysa did the same, curling up in the bedroll she shared with Ethne. Liadan had first watch, but Ethne decided to stay up with her. And so, the two knights sat together around the fire in silence.

Ethne thought Liadan had become very quiet since the Valley of Queens – quieter than usual, anyway.

"Spill it," Ethne said as soon as she heard Lysa's soft snores. She and Liadan were sitting on rocks around the fire, gauntlets off, and Liadan was still eating a chunk of old bread. Ethne had a skin of wine in hand, which she'd nicked off Rowan back at Hilvara's Knickers.

"Spill what?" said Liadan, staring at the fire. She took a big bite of bread and chewed, still not looking at Ethne. "I told you everything the armless man told me. I swear it by the gods."

"Not the armless man!" Ethne made an impatient face. "There's something else, and you can't hide whatever it is from me. I've known you since we were fourteen!"

That was true. While Liadan had been sent to the academy as a little child, Ethne hadn't been exiled and disowned until she was a teenager and had infuriated a nobleman by bedding his daughter. All her hopes and dreams of becoming a bard were dashed, her titles were stripped, and she was never to return to Fahmar Castle, her family home, again. She hadn't written her mother in months and felt terrible, but she supposed it couldn't be helped with all that was happening.

Liadan gave Ethne a sheepish look, hesitated, and said with a heavy sigh, "I believe I may have . . . impregnated Ava."

Ethne stared.

"Do not look at me like that," Liadan begged, her eyes on the fire.

Ethne thought the Knight of the Wild looked deeply ashamed, but she couldn't process what'd she'd heard. Two women . . . having a child? "Wait . . . what?" said Ethne, squinting.

Liadan sighed again. "I'm in love with Ava," she said helplessly, "and as a result, my body is trying to breed with her."

It was Ethne's turn to stare at the fire. Because of her friendship with Liadan, she knew a great deal of the customs and ways of the Wildoras women, but she had never before known that they could impregnate other women. She had always thought it a myth.

"How does Ava feel about it?" Ethne asked.

Liadan gave Ethne another helpless, strangled look. "She's happy! She took my hand and put my fingers inside her – again and again! And commanded me to make love to her! And I yielded. Old Gods, help me, I yielded."

Ethne laughed in disbelief. "Then what is the problem?!"

Liadan shook her head. "I knew you wouldn't understand!" she said irritably. "Don't you see? She will become large with child while we are running from danger and sleeping in the snow and mud – How could a child survive all of this?! It will have perished after one day." Liadan dropped her bread and buried her face in her hands.

Frowning in sympathy, Ethne reached over and clapped a comforting had on Liadan's shoulder. "Liadan, you are not alone in this, my friend. I shall help you! We shall find a place for Ava to give birth, and your child shall live! This I swear!"

Liadan glanced up and smiled gratefully. "What did I do to become worthy of such loyalty?"

"Remember when Estrid kept handing my ass to me as a lark? And you beat the shite out of her, and she stopped?"

"Yes."

"Figured I owed you for that."

Liadan laughed. "What would I do without you?"

"Probably panic and eat your own arm," said Ethne, returning her thoughtful gaze to the fire. "Liadan . . . do you *want* children?"

Liadan smiled wistfully. "Yes. And I want them with Ava, or my body wouldn't be having this reaction to her. It's just, the timing is off. So incredibly off."

"You keep saying that," said Ethne, "but we have nine months . . . don't we?" she asked when Liadan looked at her unhappily.

"Wildoras pregnancies can take as little as a few weeks," said Liadan wretchedly.

"Shite," muttered Ethne.

Liadan nodded heavily in agreement.

"No wonder there are so many of you," Ethne realized. "Well, don't worry. Hastow isn't far from here. We'll get Ava there, and what better place to give birth than the temple of the goddess of love . . .?" Ethne trailed off when she saw the look of horror on Liadan's face and remembered that Liadan did not venerate the New Gods but the Old. "Oh, shite . . . sorry."

"My child shall be born in the temple of a goddess I am not sworn to," said Liadan heavily, "far from the sheltering trees of my Wildoras."

"Perhaps we should stay in Wildoras after we've crossed the bridge," suggested Ethne. "Let Ava have the child there, if it means so much. I mean, it's not like the dragon egg is even hatched. Your people don't need to know about it."

Liadan shook her head. "We did promise Rowan and Saoirse to attend their wedding. And Ava reveres the goddess Eyslath, as all her people do. She is the one birthing the child, so she is the one who decides. I believe she would rather give birth in the care of her own goddess, though she will not admit it. And I feel compelled, as ever, to please her."

"Well, shite."

"The New Gods shall curse me for this, perhaps curse my children—"

"Don't be ridiculous," said Ethne at once. "What sort of gods would curse children?"

Liadan gave her a withering look. "Clearly, you hath not paid much attention to your own people's teachings. The goddess Hilvara alone did turn a child to gold, and there are other such tales of the New Gods taking children to the underworld or turning them to rats."

Ethne laughed. She had never believed in any of the stories about the gods whether Old or New and had always thought Liadan's devotion a little ridiculous. But Liadan's faith was a part of the reason she only made love to women she cared about. She loved Ava, she was fond of Lysa (if not occasionally annoyed by her), and the woman they had bedded together in Thurid had been a good friend who they had known for years when they were but youths.

Ethne was still hoping she and Liadan both could lay with Lysa someday. She was not angry that Lysa had slept with Liadan. She was angry that Lysa had slept with Liadan *while Ethne was in a jailcell.* Some days she still couldn't believe that Lysa had done such a thing while Ethne was far away, being beaten by ruffians and fearing for her life. It was as if she meant nothing to the handmaiden at all. Meanwhile, she had gotten on her knees and begged in earnest for Lysa's love. She often asked herself what was becoming of her. No woman had ever made a fool of her like this before.

"And what of you and Lysa," said Liadan, picking up her bread from the cave floor. "Shall you have children one day?"

Ethne snorted. "I don't know if you've been paying attention, Liadan, but Lysa has no intention whatsoever of becoming a family woman! All she talks about is slaying things and going on grand adventures! It sounds fun, if I am honest, and I think I shall go with her, when all of this is over."

"If she'll have you," teased Liadan.

Ethne grinned. "Aye. If she'll have me. Something tells me she will."

"Aye. Can't imagine she would turn down a personal servant."

"*Or,*" Ethne shot back, "perhaps my tongue is ecstasy and my fingers heaven."

Quite amused, Liadan rolled her eyes, brushed off the bread, and took another bite.

ETHNE HAD NEVER BEFORE considered having children, but once the idea was put in her head, she could think of little else. They stayed in the cave, hiding from the blizzard for another day and a night, and during all that time, Ethne daydreamed of a domestic life with Lysa, somewhere in the green hills of Tur or the countryside of Virinas.

One night as she was on watch, Ethne took off her gauntlets and crawled into her bedroll beside Lysa. Lysa was sleeping soundly on her side when Ethne gently gathered the small woman in her arms and held her from behind, sitting up against a rock. Lysa moaned and her lashes fluttered as she awoke to find herself seated between Ethne's legs.

"What are you up to?" Lysa scolded, peering over her shoulder at Ethne. "You're supposed to be on watch!"

"I *am* on watch," returned Ethne. "I can watch the cave entrance and your tits at the same time."

Lysa made an impatient, scoffing noise, though Ethne knew she was pleased by her words.

Ethne closed her arms around Lysa, hugging her from behind. "Fairest Lysa," she said and hesitated.

Lysa frowned, twisting in Ethne's arms to look up at her. "Why do I get the feeling you are about to propose to me? Are . . . are you *blushing*?"

Ethne bit her lip in embarrassment: her cheeks were indeed quite hot. "Why must you make everything so difficult?" she complained. "I want to know. . . That is . . ."

"If this is about Ava's pregnancy," said Lysa, making Ethne go still, "I already know, for she hath told me, and *no*, I do not wish for children!"

"Why not?" asked Ethne, crestfallen.

Lysa looked up at Ethne in amazement. "As if every feminine woman should wish for them?"

"That's not what I meant!" said Ethne quickly.

"I am going to go on adventures," said Lysa firmly, "slaying dragons and giants! I shall have no time for children!"

"What about when you are old and frail and can no longer go on adventures?"

"When I am old and frail, I suspect I shall have no patience for children," Lysa returned. She made an impatient noise again. "You are only pursuing this because of Liadan! You must mimic everything she does! If Liadan didn't want children, you would not!"

"I . . . that isn't true," said Ethne helplessly, though she very much knew it was true.

"It is sweet of you to want a family with me," said Lysa in a softer voice. She reached up and touched Ethne's face, and when she gazed up at the knight, her brown eyes were warm with affection. Ethne's heart skipped a happy beat.

"But it simply isn't what I want," finished Lysa.

"What do you want?" Ethne whispered and gazed down at Lysa intently, as if she would run out into the storm and return with the throne of Illa if Lysa but asked.

Lysa appeared pleased and flustered, but she composed herself and answered wistfully, "I want to see the seven kingdoms! I want to travel the realms, fight monsters, lay with beautiful women, and drink wine until I pass out! And I want to do it for a good fifty years! Perhaps even a little after my breasts sag."

Ethne chuckled. "Sounds like fun. Shall I come along?"

"Perhaps. If you behave yourself," said Lysa, playfully regal.

Ethne gave a half-smile. "But you like it when I misbehave . . ." she whispered, and her eyes went to the naked flesh of Lysa's neck and collarbone.

Lysa went still when Ethne gently tugged at the buckles of her leather chest guard until it fell away, revealing her tunic. Ethne's careful hands then pried at the laces of Lysa's tunic and tugged it down around her shoulders, until her breasts had pushed free of the fabric. They were small breasts, but they were plump and swollen and so perky. Ethne squeezed them carefully in both hands and saw the little pink nipples harden, jutting from the plump mounds. She massaged again, watching the soft breasts give in her careful fingers, and she heard Lysa moan softly, her head falling back.

Ethne's hands moved down to the belt of Lysa's tight trousers, and she unbuckled it, then tugged at the buttons, until Lysa's trousers sagged open, revealing her linen panties. Ethne's hand slid down the front of Lysa's panties and touched her sex. The soft lips were fat with desire; the brown, curly pubic hair was moist with Lysa's arousal.

Gazing up at Ethne breathlessly, Lysa's cheeks blushed a little and she shivered as she was fingered. Ethne, careful and slow, plunged her fingers through Lysa's heat and moisture while massaging one of her breasts. She watched for a time as Lysa melted in her grasp, caught between her armored legs there on the cave floor, as the fire danced nearby.

As Lysa grew wetter, Ethne's fingers slid deeper, harder – but just as slow as before. Lysa trembled and bit her lip to silence a moan, terrified Ava and Liadan would awake. She dropped her head back in silent ecstasy, her pretty brown eyes suffering when they gazed up at Ethne. Ethne looked at Lysa's sweet pink lips, and as she made gentle love to her, she leaned down and kissed her tenderly on the mouth.

Chapter 4

Ethne didn't know what was happening to her, but after making love to Lysa and watching the small woman shiver and climax in her arms, she had decided that she could not let Lysa go, could never leave her side, and that they must be wed one way or the other.

The next morning, the storm finally lifted, and as they walked from the cave, heading always south toward Godga and the river, Ethne walked at the front of the procession with Liadan while Lysa and Ava walked some feet behind them, whispering and giggling excitedly. Ethne assumed they were giggling about Ava's pregnancy or perhaps her pending marriage to Liadan. Liadan and Ava had been talking about marriage for days – not with each other but to their respective best friends – and it was driving Ethne to distraction with wild thoughts. Ethne wanted to make Lysa hers and keep others from stealing her heart. Somehow, her closest friends – Liadan and Rowan – had both managed to do so with their women, and it was driving Ethne mad trying to figure it out.

"Does Ava know she's supposed to propose to you? That it's your people's custom?" Ethne asked Liadan, as behind them another bought of giggles erupted.

"I haven't told her," Liadan said with a shrug. "What's important right now is reaching Godga before Luane finds us again."

"Entering the Valley of Queens was clever, I'll admit," said Ethne thoughtfully. "Luane wouldn't know about the escape tunnel in Queen

Saraid's tomb . . . Or rather, the tunnel that was built to bring in a damned dragon corpse. Ha."

"Luane will wander for a time, trying to pick up our trail, though it will have stopped on the edge of the valley, which contains thousands of tombs. Make no mistake, though, Ethne: she *will* find us again."

"Not before we reach Godga," said Ethne with determination. "And we shall be ready. It's not like the old hag is far away. Hell, we'd have already been to the river if not for the horses abandoning us."

"True enough," agreed Liadan.

Ethne was right of course: a line of trees had already appeared in the distance, and the gleam of the ice-plated river shone in the sunlight. Before long, they would have reached Godga's little cabin, where she lived beside the great stone Bridge of Breandan. Ethne had a foreboding feeling about all of it, but she knew protesting was pointless, so determined were the others in their quest, and so she changed the subject back to their more present worries.

Ethne glanced sideways at Liadan, who was glowering in silent contemplation. "Why do you fear Luane so greatly?" she asked with sudden exasperation. "I mean, I *know* she is 'the Dragon,' but you are one of the fiercest warriors I ever did see! And I grew up in Adwean, where the great tourneys are held, and all the greatest warriors come year after year to compete. I have seen true skill, and you have it."

Liadan smiled sadly. "Perhaps. But my skills have never before been tested, Ethne! Our training was just that – training. It was not the real world, where warriors die on the end of blades. We did only graduate this past fall, and I have only tested my strength against meager bandits and cutthroats."

"That is not true," said Ethne at once. "We have slain giants, orcs, and goblins—"

"While Saoirse, our instructor, aided us and kept us from real harm," Liadan finished for her.

"Fine!" said Ethne, frustrated. "I'll give you that. But you shall not face Luane alone, Liadan! I shall aid you. And I suppose Lysa shall as well. She hath insisted on it, in fact." Ethne spoke the last words with great bitterness.

Liadan's lips twitched, threatening to blossom into a smile. She was holding back for Ethne's sake, Ethne could tell: Ethne *hated* the idea of Lysa fighting and it was a sensitive subject for her.

"For weeks we have traveled with Lysa and still you hath not tamed her?" Liadan said, apparently unable to resist teasing after all.

Ethne sighed. "More like she hath tamed me. I'm starting to find it difficult to even look at other women – me! And I used to bed two women a night!"

Liadan chuckled.

"She is on my mind night and day, she haunts my thoughts, she plagues my dreams," went on Ethne, "and if they were not such sweet dreams, filled with kisses and laughter, I should despise her. But she is just as sweet when I am awake, with her doting brown eyes and smirking lips. And how she loves to seduce me, always letting her tunic drape about her cleavage. I shall go mad before long."

"By the *gods*, has she got you around her little finger. Not that I have room to talk," said Liadan. "Ava doth command me without a second thought, and I do enjoy kneeling ever before her."

Ethne laughed. "Of course, you do. Lysa hath told me of your 'kneeling.'"

Liadan laughed as well.

"Perhaps if I could . . . capture her somehow. Tell me how it is done, Liadan," Ethne implored. "You and Rowan both somehow managed to bind Ava and Saoirse to you. How? What words did you speak to them?"

"Perhaps you're just terrible in bed," said Liadan with a shrug.

Ethne scowled impatiently. "Do not jest!"

"Why are you so determined to wed Lysa?" Liadan asked tiredly. "She already loves thee. Isn't that enough?"

"No, it's not enough," Ethne said at once. "I don't want her to give her love to another. I want her to be mine, always, my companion and my love. She may lay with as many women as she doth please. It is her heart I fear losing."

Liadan sighed. "Ethne . . . if Lysa falls in love with another, a wedding band on her finger will not stay her heart."

Ethne gazed unhappily at the ground as they walked. "I know . . . but if she doth decide to leave me for another, at least I shall legally own half of what she doth own!"

Liadan laughed.

"That, to me, is worth the trouble of a wedding band," went on Ethne. "She will not be able to abandon me so easily."

Liadan chuckled again, her deep voice rising louder. "All right, all right," she said. "I shall give you my advice, though you are a bard and could have thought of such romantic gestures yourself."

"I never completed my bard training, you know that," returned Ethne, "and bard training does not include instructions on wooing fair maidens. . . not on purpose, anyway. Do tell me. I would take notes if only I had quill and ink."

Liadan shook her head, amused. "Well, Lysa doth like jewelry. Didn't you notice? When next we are in town, have something custom made for her, something that will match her eyes. Maidens do love such gestures."

"Really? Have you done the same for Ava?"

"Aye. When we were still at Caradin, I used to bring her winter flowers every morning from the courtyard. Just one flower, though. I didn't want anyone to notice what I was doing. Many thought the flower was for myself, as I did pin it to my armor."

Ethne laughed. "Clever."

It was then that Ava and Lysa jogged up, walking beside Ethne and Liadan. Ava slid her arm in Liadan's, and Lysa did likewise with Ethne. Ethne thought the women looked pink-cheeked and mischievous. They were flushed with happiness and excitement. It made her feel wary. The last time they had looked that way, they had concocted yet another way to torment Ethne sexually: they had bathed in front of Ethne back in their room at the tavern while Liadan slept, but both had refused to lay with Ethne afterwards, leaving in her a throbbing hell of quiet passion. The vixens.

"What are the two of you up to?" said Ethne, eyes narrowed suspiciously.

"Never you mind," said Lysa, looking quite pleased with herself. Her eyes went to the bridge and the river, at both landmarks taking shape in the distance, and she became thoughtful. "I suppose we're almost there. Perhaps Luane will attack while we wait there, and then we can put this madness to an end."

"Why are you so certain that Luane shall find us at Godga's cabin?" Liadan demanded wearily. "It would make a clever trap if there were certainty to it."

"But there *is* certainty," said Lysa at once. "Think about it. Why would Luane pursue you to Hastow? She doesn't know about your sister there! She would assume you would head to the bridge, head home, and pursue us here. Unless she's a complete muttonhead."

"*Is* Luane a muttonhead?" Ava wondered. "That could work to our advantage."

Lysa snorted. "She's a muttonhead if I ever saw. She'll fall into this trap. Her arrogance will do her in."

"Don't be so quick to assume, fair Lysa," said Ethne with a sigh. "Big doesn't always equate stupid, and dragons were not always the dumb beasts they are now. They were clever once. Queen Saraid's dragon, for instance, was called Ethicar. It could talk, even aided with battle planning and strategy."

"That's right, you're a bard," said Ava, remembering, and Ethne thought she sounded pleased. "You would know the tales of my house. I'd wager you learned all of the songs of House Damaris."

"Only some of them, your highness," Ethne answered. "As you'll recall, I did not complete my training. I am a knight first and foremost, even if my tongue doth carry sweet melodies. Sweet Lysa, I have played you like a flute, have I not? And my, did you *sing*." She glanced sideways at Lysa and was very pleased with herself when Lysa blushed.

"Stop tormenting fair Lysa," chuckled Liadan. "You'll make her wet her pants."

"Easy enough way to get her out of them," returned Ethne, enjoying it when Lysa blushed brighter. "It's a shame the river's frozen. We could have bathed. I do hate walking about covered in stale sweat and soot. Soot from magick fire is always terrible."

"But you are not so filthy that Lysa would not have you," said Liadan, amused. "I heard the two of you this morning."

Lysa was red enough to rival a tomato now. "You d-did?"

Ava giggled. "Stop, the pair of you! You'll give dear Lysa a heart attack! Pay them no mind, Lysa."

"I don't know why she should be embarrassed," said Ethne. "She hath lain with all three of us."

Liadan chuckled again. "She is not embarrassed. She is aroused."

Lysa didn't answer: Liadan was right.

Liadan nodded at the great stone bridge as it took shape ahead. "Why is it called the Breandan Bridge, then?"

"For my ancestor," said Ava before Ethne could answer, and the others looked around at her, surprised yet again that she knew any history.

"Breandan was one of the first queens of Isline, the seven realms," went on Ava. "She was a wild woman who hailed from Wildoras. She fell in love with one of the fairest women in Illa and married her. Afterwards, she lived in Illa the rest of her life. The people there loved her, and she became the first queen of the land. She built Caradin Castle for her wife—they named it after their daughter—and she built the bridge to open a trade route between Wildoras and Illa, uniting the two realms."

"During that time," Ethne added, "Wildoras was a thriving land, with great stone buildings that rose to the heavens, paved streets, and bursting forests and fields. It was the richest country in the land—"

"And now my people sleep in the mud and hunt the boar like cave dwellers," said Liadan quietly, and Ethne could tell she regretted asking about the bridge.

"So why is everyone unable to cross the bridge now?" Lysa wondered.

"Well, with the fall of Wildoras, people began to hate and fear the magi," said Ava. "You must remember, the curse was placed on them because they abused their power. Angry mobs would go into Wildoras and burn their villages to the ground, even if it meant they were massacred by angry Wildorans. Eventually, the wild women put up a barrier to keep people out and themselves in."

"And Godga somehow became the guardian of the bridge? Is she even a Wildoran?" Lysa prompted.

"Who the hell knows what Godga is?" said Ethne. "One reason why we shouldn't be heading south."

"You keep saying that," said Lysa irritably, "but where else would we go?"

"To Hastow," said Ethne at once. "Saoirse would slay the Dragon for us—"

"And die just days before her wedding day in the process," said Liadan darkly. "We are going to Godga, Ethne. Let that be an end to it."

Ethne took a great, shuddering breath but held her tongue. She knew Liadan was frightened of endangering the people of Hastow, but she herself was more of a pragmatist. She was willing to do whatever it took to survive, the casualties be damned. Her greatest fear was watching Lysa die and being helpless to stop it.

A copse of trees blocked their way forward, and it was here that they were suddenly ambushed – not by the Dragon of Almara but by orcs! The green warriors were tall, muscular women, with tusks poking from fat bottom lips, black eyes, and wild black hair. They wore ragged furs and carried heavy two-handed weapons: crude and chipped battle-axes, clubs, and great swords. There were only three of them, but being seven feet tall and as supernaturally strong as any Wildoran, they might as well have been ten.

Liadan reacted immediately, throwing out her hand and sending a ball of golden fire into the face of the nearest orc, who growled angrily and toppled over on her back in the snow, dropping her battle-axe and flailing as she clutched her burning face. In only a few seconds, she was dead.

Seeing their comrade down, the remaining two orcs snorted furiously and charged. One ran at Ava, battle-axe lifted, tusks drippling with strings of drool. Ava – stricken with fear – stood paralyzed as the great battle-axe swung down at her face. The blade halted just inches from her forehead, parried by Liadan's flaming blade. Liadan kicked the orc back, her expression cold, and as the two of them fell into a fierce struggle, the second orc was locked in battle with Ethne, who – lacking any super strength such as Liadan and the orcs possessed – was not doing as well.

"You leave her alone!" yelled Lysa, ripping her sword from its sheath, but compared to the great two-handed sword the orc was wielding, Lysa might as well have been brandishing a butterknife. The orc actually stopped in her tracks and guffawed with laughter, her deep voice echoing through the trees. While the green woman was distracted, Ethne lunged in an attempt to stab, but the orc's reflexes were swift: she brought her great sword around in a mighty arc, parrying off the blow and slicing Ethne through her vambrace. Ethne grunted and staggered back in a splash of blood, dropping her blade and sitting hard in the snow.

"Ethne!" Lysa screamed, horrified. Her face twisting, she turned on orc and lunged into battle with her.

Panting and clutching her wounded arm, Ethne watched through strings of hair, watched in amazement as little Lysa – fast and fierce –

dodged, parried, and sliced at the giant roaring orc who towered over her. She was so quick and small, the big, slow orc simply couldn't keep up, and it wasn't long before the snorting green woman had fallen to one knee, completely baffled as she bled from the many vicious cuts Lysa had given her.

Eyes blazing, Lysa pirouetted and took off the orc's head. The head (its expression comically shocked) went flying through the cold air and landed in the snow, where it bounced away, trailing blood. The big, headless, green body collapsed over in a toss of snow, the neck squirting blood. Lysa stood over her defeated enemy for a moment, panting and sweating from her efforts, and Ethne looked up at her in her tight leather armor, her brown hair wild, thinking Lysa was so beautiful and strong – more beautiful and strong than Ethne had ever realized. All that fierceness in that little body, and Ethne had reduced her to a "peasant" who cleaned chamber pots.

Eventually, Lysa turned to Ethne, and her frightened brown eyes were full of tears as she said hoarsely, "Are you all right? I thought she would kill you for certain!"

Ethne laughed weakly. "As ever, your confidence in me is staggering, my lady."

Lysa rolled her eyes, all the concern and fear vanishing with her irritation. She wiped her red blade clean on the snow, sheathed it again, and helped Ethne to her feet.

Ethne glanced around and saw Liadan hugging Ava tight and stroking her golden hair. Ava's face had nearly been cleaved in two and she was sobbing and shaken by what had nearly happened. Liadan was shushing Ava and soothing her . . . but she kept glancing at Lysa, and Ethne knew she was impressed by the little handmaiden, perhaps even as aroused as Ethne herself was. In that moment, Ethne decided they would most definitely have to make a go at Lysa, the two of them.

Lysa didn't notice anyone's lusting, though. She was focused on Ethne's injury. Her eyes danced unhappily over Ethne's bloody arm, and the concern had returned.

Ethne could hear her own heart thundering in her ears. She was going to do something impulsive, she knew it. She had never wanted Lysa more than she did in that moment. Thoughts of yanking her pants down and tasting her were overwhelming.

"You're hurt!" Lysa said wretchedly. "You're hurt because I insisted we come –Mmph!"

Ethne suddenly kissed Lysa hard on the mouth. Lysa stiffened in shock but very quickly melted into the kiss. She was trembling and breathless when Ethne pulled away and said, "Lysa, will you marry me?"

Chapter 5

Ava thought Ethne was out of her mind, asking Lysa to marry her. Lysa seemed to have every intention of becoming a great adventurer and only seemed half-serious about her courtship with Ethne. Ava thought it odd: in the beginning, everyone had assumed that Ethne – being a lecher – was the one who did not take their budding romance as anything real. But it was Ethne who wanted commitment and partnership, it was Ethne who wanted marriage, while Lysa dreamed only of traveling, treasure hunting, and bedding women. It would have been funny if Ethne's heart wasn't being dragged through the mud, Ava thought.

As they were walking that morning, some time before the orc attack, Lysa had confided in secret that she did indeed care for Ethne, but she wasn't ready to settle down. She then went on to describe all the things she wanted to do – including a few of the women she planned to return to Hargendon to bed and the things she wanted to do to them. Ava had giggled her head off, delighted by how naughty her former handmaiden was.

Lysa then confessed that she was excited to visit Hastow not just for the wedding but in order to see Rowan again. While she did care for Ethne, she had desired big, strong, laughing Rowan something fierce and admitted that the two of them had kissed on more than one occasion, with Rowan even touching her breasts.

Ava had to admit she was a little jealous. She and Lysa had both been locked away at Caradin for most of their lives, never seeing other women who were like them, and now that they were out, it seemed only Lysa was having any real fun! Every time Ava tried to have fun, it blew up in her face. She sometimes still thought of the man at Hilvara's Knickers with burning fury. Bedding Saoirse had been pleasant, at least, but knowing that the Knight of the Lion *also* preferred Lysa irked Ava as well. The way Saoirse had looked at Lysa – as if Lysa were a savory morsel she wanted to devour! Ava wanted the knights to look at her that way. She was supposed to be a classical beauty – a lovely princess with long, golden hair—but it seemed only Liadan really wanted her – and even *Liadan* lusted for Lysa, she knew.

It was getting to a point where, if Liadan tried bedding Ava and Lysa both again, Ava would not allow it.

With the orcs dead, they paused to bandage Ethne's cut arm – Lysa fussing over the Knight of the Sparrow all the while – and then they continued on to Godga's cabin. It was a small cabin standing under two large trees, both of them naked of leaves, their scraggly branches reaching like death's fingers to the sky. To Ava's shock, there were bones and severed heads hanging from the cabin rafters, and the skull of a young dragon stood outside near the step, just large enough to match the size of a wooden chair.

Noticing the dragon skull with horror, Ava decided to hide her dragon egg inside her cloak, away from Godga's prying eyes. She was terrified the old witch would try to take it.

As they drew nearer, Ava thought the entire area surrounding Godga's cabin was eerie. Here, there was no birdsong, and the sky seemed ever overcast with gray, and even the whisper of the lake beneath the ice wasn't soothing but rather sounded like the whispers of the dead. Dark, gloomy, and cold – in the middle of the day! It gave Ava a terrible, foreboding feeling, but she also knew they had come too far to turn back now. Godga was their only chance.

"So here we are," said Ethne unhappily. "Now is our last chance to turn back. We don't have to do this."

"There is no turning back," Ava said, startled by the finality in her own voice. But she could feel it, something closing behind her, as if she had reached a point of no return. Whatever happened after this – whether she drove out King Bjorn or not—would result directly from having come here, she knew.

Ava squared her shoulders, lifted her chin, and wiggling from Liadan's protecting arm, she strolled toward the wooden front door of the cabin and knocked three times. She heard the others crunching over the snow behind her, heard Ethne muttering bitterly under her breath that they should turn back.

There was movement and shuffling on the other side. Then the door opened, and they all looked down into the wrinkled face of a tiny old woman, who stood before them wrapped in fur shawls and wearing a ragged peasant's gown. Her long hair fell around her in a silvery veil, and her small eyes were quick and cunning. She smiled at them quite suddenly, showing gaps in her crooked, black teeth. Behind Ava, Lysa gasped, appalled.

"I've been waiting for you, Daughter of Breandan," said Godga, gazing up at Ava with a sort of hunger that unsettled her.

The old woman's foul breath hit Ava full in the face, and she tried not to sneer as she answered, "Waiting for me?"

"Yessss," said Godga, hissing like a snake. Her smile was wide, her greedy eyes still fixed on Ava. Very slowly, her black eyes moved to Liadan, and she said with approval, "Hmm. Yesss. And the wild woman. . . ." Her eyes moved to Ethne and Lysa, who stiffened. "And the Sparrow and the pirate queen. Yesss."

Lysa frowned. "I'm not a . . ."

"Come in, won't you?" said Godga, bowing and standing aside as she held open the door.

They filed inside, and Godga closed the door behind them, shutting out the cold.

"Sit and eat," said the Godga. "Sit! Sit!"

Ava stood still for a moment, relieved as the heat of the room washed over her. A fire was roaring on the hearth, and wooden cups of water and bowls of hot stew had been set out on a wooden table set for four. Ava frowned at the table. The Godga had known they were coming, but how? The last Seer had died a thousand years before. Or so the stories said.

"Sit!" Godga practically screeched, impatient now.

Ava and the others finally went to the table and sat, and the knights took off their gauntlets. They glanced around the cozy little room, from which branched a hall, but it looked like a normal cabin any old peasant woman would have lived in: cooking utensils and pots hanging from the rafters, a brace of hares drying, a few chairs near the fire. Except there were skulls and bones here, too. Human and orc skulls—and what looked like a few small goblin skulls – hung from the ceiling, grinning with yellow teeth.

Godga took one of the skulls down, and they saw her ladle some stew from the cauldron simmering on the edge of the fire. Then she sat at the table with them and – to Ava's horror – started drinking the stew from the skull.

"Eat! Eat!" Godga cried, pausing irritably when she noticed they weren't eating but staring at her.

They all hesitated, then deciding there was no reason for the Magi Godga to poison them, they started eating. Ava found the stew surprisingly delicious.

"The Dragon of Almara will be here soon," the Godga said, startling them all so that they stopped eating and looked at her. The Godga was staring at the ceiling, as if she was listening to something distant, and her pale lips were parted. After another beat, she looked around the table at them and said gleefully, "Ah yesss. She comes. She comes!" She gave a surprisingly girlish giggle.

Liadan frowned. "Will you stop the Dragon? We came to you for aid."

"Yes, I will stop her," said Godga calmly.

Ava looked up quickly. "You will?" she asked sharply. "But why? How does it benefit you to aid us? There must be a reason you agreed so quickly."

Godga smiled, showing her horrible teeth again. "Ooo. You ask the smart questions. Not as stupid as I thought you were."

Ava's face darkened.

"I don't think any of you could comprehend just how old I am or *who* I am," said Godga seriously, almost sternly, "so suffice it to say that I remember a time when elves walked this land and when women ruled in peace and prosperity. Since the men took over, it has been constant war, trouble, and strife. I would see an end to that." She looked at Ava. "*You* are the key to restoring the world to what it once was. You are the last living female descendant of House Damaris! If I help you survive, you will find yourself able to return and take back your throne."

"Yes!" Ava said at once, suddenly breathless as the yearning overtook her. "That is exactly what I desire! I don't know how I shall gather an army, but there must be those who still support my claim."

"You will not need an army," said Godga.

Everyone at the table went still, and Ava knew they were thinking of her dragon egg.

Ethne squinted. "What do you mean?"

"I *mean*," said Godga, her eyes sliding to their corners to regard Ethne irritably, "the princess will hatch her dragon egg!"

The dragon egg was hidden behind Ava's cloak still, and she clutched it protectively in one arm, letting her cloak fall back to reveal it. So the Godga already knew, then.

"And she will give birth to a mighty daughter – Mightier than the Dragon of Almara herself!" Godga went on triumphantly. "And this daughter will return to the seven kingdoms and take them for women. And Ava, once queen, will have a second daughter – and she will give it to me."

"What!" Ava cried at once. It took her a moment to realize Liadan had shouted the same word.

Godga's calm expression didn't change. She was sipping from her skull of stew and waved a dismissive hand. "You would only have to give me the one, not the both of them," she said, as if this should have soothed them.

Ava placed a protective hand over her womb, in which Liadan's fiery seed was still blazing. She glared across the table at the old woman.

Liadan scowled. "Never! You shall never have a child of mine! You hag!"

Godga only smiled at the insult and continued sipping her stew. She was looking at Ava and she was waiting, almost as if she knew what was going through Ava's mind.

Ava bit her lip, knowing that she was relenting. She wanted to return to Caradin Castle. She wanted her dresses and her pretty things, she wanted to rule the seven realms on high, and she wanted to see the age of men crumble to dust. And after sleeping for weeks on the hard, cold ground and starving on what food they could get between taverns, she was willing to pay any price at this point, any price. She could feel the disbelief of the others, how they stared at her with their mouths open, their eyes large, as she said, "What would you do with my child – the child?"

"Ava!" Liadan cried in disbelief.

"You can't be serious!" Lysa hissed, leaning toward Ava.

Godga only smiled smugly. "I am all alone in this cabin. Powerful as I am, the one thing I cannot do is bear children. I wish to pass my knowledge on, raise another magi to guard the bridge."

Lysa scowled. "The bridge won't need guarding when the age of women is restored!"

Godga's small, black eyes slid to Lysa. "Won't it? Restoring the balance will awaken old things . . . Dragons, giants, beings that have slumbered since the fall of woman . . . the Old Gods. The magick will come pouring out of Wildoras, chaotic and unchecked, if there is no one here to hold it back. I have been the sentinel for centuries. My time is almost spent."

"Why didn't you have your own daughter then?" Ava demanded. Her hand was still clutched protectively over her womb.

"I did," said Godga quietly. "She is dead."

Silence fell over the table, and Godga calmly sipped stew from her skull again, not looking at anyone.

"But wait," said Ava into the silence, "I thought the women of Wildoras were cursed, that women were no longer allowed to rule after what the wild women did."

Godga shook her head. "The gods never cursed anyone, child. And the Wildorans never abused their power! Those are fairytales! It was men – King Azmon specifically – who cursed women. He was jealous of our power, and so he sought to cast us down." Her face twisted with bitterness and disgust.

Ava's face darkened, remembering the story. Yes, Azmon had been responsible for the fall of women. She had been taught that much, even if the rest had been lies.

"Of course, the notion that King Azmon could wield magick was another lie," went on Godga scathingly. "No man has ever wielded magick! Azmon could not have lit a candle! No, he summoned four beings of darkness and sent them forth to the four corners of the realms, and there, each being guards a great crystal in a tower, and each crystal holds the curse in place over all women."

"So to break the curse," said Ethne, "someone would have to kill those monsters and destroy the crystals. . ." She sighed. "Is that someone us?"

Godga grinned, amused by Ethne's lack of enthusiasm. "If the princess would restore the realms to women, yes. Of course," she waved a wrinkled hand, "the princess could just as easily take her own throne and forget the other kingdoms. But that is not your intention, is it, Princess Ava Damaris, fifth of your name?"

Ava regally lifted her chin, pleased to hear her title. She looked at Liadan imploringly. "Will you help me in this, my love?"

"The answer is in the question," said Liadan with a smile. "I am yours, my princess." She reached across the table and took Ava's hand. "To the very end."

Ava's heart fluttered.

"I can't believe it!" burst Lysa happily, making them all jump. Her fists were clenched under her chin, and she was grinning widely, her brown eyes almost feverish. "We're going on a quest!!!"

AS IT TURNED OUT, THE Magi Godga was right about Luane arriving there. Shortly after they had finished eating, the Dragon of Almara sent a fireball at the cabin. Ava watched in horror as a giant ball of flame came rocketing at the window – while Godga calmly sipped from her skull and did not look up – and was amazed when the fireball bounced harmlessly off the glass and sprang back at Luane – hitting her in the face. Luane fell to the snow, where she writhed in agony, consumed by her own fire. They all sat in the cabin, listening awkwardly, as she burned to death.

"There's a protection charm over the cabin," Godga calmly explained when they all looked to her.

Lysa looked smugly at Ethne. "Told you she was a muttonhead."

Ethne rolled her eyes and tipped back her cup for a gulp of water.

When Luane's screams quieted, Liadan looked across the table at Ava, and her blue eyes were sad.

"What is it, my knight?" Ava asked, rubbing Liadan's hand soothingly.

Liadan shook her head. "It is cowardly that I hid in here while Luane fell into a trap. Cowardly and without honor!"

Ethne made an impatient noise. "Oh, get over yourself, Liadan! Would you rather have died facing her? Because that's what would have happened! Letting Luane make a jest of herself was the smarter path."

"Glad you see things my way now," agreed Lysa, still looking smug.

Ethne shrugged. "It's true I wanted to journey to Hastow, but I'm glad we could spare Saoirse this fight. She's getting too old for this shite anyhow."

Ava rose gracefully from the table, meeting eyes with old Godga, who looked up at her with a small smile. "Thank you for your aid," Ava said graciously. "When our second child is old enough to walk, I s-shall return her here to become your apprentice, though it tears my hair in twain to do so."

Godga's smile widened, though it did not go to her cold black eyes. "I shall hold you to your promise . . . *your highness.*"

Ava looked into the black voids of Godga's eyes and thought she perceived something of a threat. But the look was gone as quickly as it'd come, and then they were out in the snow again, making their way on foot – at last – to Hastow.

More From Ash Gray

Her First Knight

Book 5

Sanctuary

Chapter 1

Soon after the Dragon of Almara had fallen prey to her own foolishness, the blizzard lifted completely, and clear blue skies spread their warmth over the snowbanks. A rainbow even appeared, shimmering innocently above, so that Ava pointed at it and giggled girlishly.

Walking beside Ethne, Lysa smiled gratefully at the rainbow in the sunny sky, reflecting that it would be spring soon and farmers would begin a new crop. The markets would be bursting, and cattle would be roaming the fields. Spring was her favorite time of year.

As they traveled down the road back toward Hastow, Lysa was still in shock that Ava was so willing to give up her own child just to retake her throne. In all the years she had known Ava, the princess had never cared about politics or ruling. It was as if entering the tomb of Queen Saraid had changed something in Ava forever, and now, there was no going back for her: she must become queen of Illa.

Liadan likewise seemed to have become determined to set Ava on the throne and was overwhelmed with the realization that she would rule the seven realms at Ava's side. The two of them could be seen sitting together at the campfire, cooing over the dragon egg – almost as if it were more their child than the actual babe growing in Ava's womb!

And that was another thing: it had been three days since Godga's cabin, and Ava was growing steadily rounder. Ethne had told Lysa that Wildoras pregnancies only took three weeks. Before long, Ava and Liadan would be parents!

It was all happening so fast. It was overwhelming to Lysa, and she was only a side observer, yet Ava and Liadan, who were directly involved, were so calm and matter-of-fact about it all.

"This is madness!" Lysa hissed at Ethne one evening when they were breaking camp.

Liadan and Ava were standing together over the fire as they warmed themselves a last time, smiling and exchanging happy whispers. Ava was still carrying the dragon egg in her makeshift sling and held it now over the flames. Lysa gasped: the silhouette of a baby dragon could be seen inside!

"What is madness?" said Ethne dismissively. "That our friends are happy? Oh, yes. Right madness that is."

Lysa glared over her shoulder at the Knight of the Sparrow. Ethne was squatting over her saddlebags and was rummaging through them as she packed them. Lysa drew near and stood over her impatiently.

"I knew you'd take her side," Lysa complained. "You don't care about anything so long as Liadan is happy."

"Yes. I'm a terrible friend," Ethne sarcastically agreed, not looking up.

Lysa scowled. "Ethne! Don't you think this is all happening too fast?"

Ethne paused and finally looked up. She was concerned now, having heard the terror in Lysa's voice. "I thought you were happy about going on a quest?" she said, confused.

"I was," Lysa admitted. "But that was before Ava said she was coming as well! Ethne, she's in no condition! Destroying the four watchtowers won't be some merry lark!" She took a halting step closer. "You *must* convince Liadan. Tell her to tell Ava to hold off this quest! At least until the babe is grown! We should away to a temple, where she may raise the child in secret. And when the child and the dragon are old enough to fend for themselves, only then should the campaign begin—"

"I have heard your counsel, fair Lysa," said Ava, startling Lysa to silence.

Lysa turned: Ava and Liadan were still standing over the fire, side by side. Ava was cradling the green dragon egg in her arms, and after being warmed over the fire, it was glittering more brightly than ever before. The brilliant color matched her eyes almost completely.

"And I shall heed it," Ava said, smiling.

Lysa hesitated. "You shall?"

"Yes," sighed Ava, who suddenly looked very tired. "I know I've been . . .hasty. It's just, it feels as if all the pieces are finally falling into place!" Her eyes glowed with excitement. "I feel like my destiny is calling me!" She glanced dotingly at Liadan (who smiled) and added, "*Our* destiny."

Liadan gazed down into Ava's doting eyes with soft affection.

Ava gazed dreamily at Liadan a moment before looking at Lysa again. "I finally understand my place in the world, and I only wish to seize it!"

Lysa shook her head. "And you *will*, princess! But not overnight!"

"As I said, I have heard your counsel, dear Lysa," Ava answered. "We shall place the quest aside, and we shall find a temple where I may give birth." She looked down at the egg in her arms. "To both my children."

Lysa paused. "Wait a minute. . . When the Godga asked for your second child. . . She meant the dragon, didn't she?"

Ava nodded unhappily. "The dragon shall help me drive out Endoreth and then . . ." She looked down at the egg sadly, and Liadan placed a comforting hand on her shoulder.

"I suppose that's better than surrendering your own child," said Lysa, relieved. She noticed tears behind Ava's eyes and was startled and confused by them: Ava was behaving as if the dragon were her actual child!

"Yes," Ava said hoarsely, though her agreement was so obviously a lie.

They broke camp and continued on foot to Hastow. Liadan and Ethne walked side by side at the head of the procession. Ethne was still carrying her saddle bags over her shoulder, and the bags jingled with the gold they had taken from Queen Saraid's tomb. Liadan walked calmly beside her, and the two knights were speaking in low voices. Lysa thought their whispered conversation seemed suspicious, for they kept glancing back at Ava and looking quickly away. What were they up to?

"Lysa, I wish to ask something of you," said Ava. She was walking beside Lysa and had been in deep contemplation for some time, gazing off at the trees ahead, her pale lashes fluttering. Now she pushed the hair behind her ear as she said, "When I am queen, I shall need an advisor." Ava waited.

Lysa hesitated, caught completely off-guard. "And you would ask me?" she said in wonder. She had to admit she was flattered.

"I know you wanted to travel and go questing," Ava said quickly, "and you could still do that! But your advice has proven quite valuable to me, and I trust you. I l-love you," she said, blushing brightly.

Lysa felt her heart flutter, and inside her leather trousers, her sex was throbbing.

"And I couldn't imagine anyone more fit to help me rule. You would forever be a part of my court—"

Lysa halted and took Ava's hands. They faced each other, and Ava blushed hotter as Lysa said, "Nothing could honor me more greatly, my princess. I love you too." So saying, Lysa bounced up on tiptoe and kissed Ava slowly on the lips.

Ava's lashes fluttered and she smiled, quite flustered and pleased.

They walked on, and now Lysa was distracted with thoughts of making sweet love to Ava. She had meditated on it often as a girl, caressing Ava's big breasts, tasting her pink sex and the soft golden hair between her thighs. And since the night Liadan had taken them, her desire had only grown twofold. Oh, what would it be like to have Ava to herself? And would Ethne care? Would it anger her? Ethne was so possessive. Lysa knew she would probably never hear the end of it. But why? It wasn't as if she and Ethne were married!

Ethne had asked days before, and Lysa still hadn't given her answer. At the time, she had assumed Ethne was joking or delirious from her battle wounds, but now Lysa was realizing exactly how serious Ethne was about marriage. The woman kept sending her longing looks, sometimes tinged with sadness. It made Lysa feel terrible.

But Lysa didn't want to marry Ethne, and she didn't want to live in Ava's court as a royal counselor! She wanted to sail a ship on the open sea, make love to many fine women, and steal gold and jewels from the rich and greedy! Since her horrible stay in Bella's room, she had not been able to get the woman's riches out of her mind. There had been so much gold and jewelry and fine things, and Bella hadn't slogged away scrubbing chamber pots to get it, either.

No. No one became rich by slaving for the rich! No one deserved to be a chambermaid! Bella had taken what the world owed her! And while Bella had been a violent monster, Lysa couldn't help admiring the carefree and lavish aspects of the pirate lifestyle. She had already decided that, once this business with Endoreth was over, she was going to join a pirate crew and live life on the sea, above and beyond the reach of the law.

They walked all night, until finally, the gray dawn crept over the horizon, reaching its long fingers between the trees. Lysa was exhausted and just thinking how wonderful it would be to make camp and lie down when Liadan said with a sigh of relief, "At last – Hastow!"

Don't miss out!

Visit the website below and you can sign up to receive emails whenever Ash Gray publishes a new book. There's no charge and no obligation.

https://books2read.com/r/B-A-ZRKF-LWEBC

Connecting independent readers to independent writers.

Also by Ash Gray

A Time of Darkness
Time's Arrow
The Infinite Athenaeum

Clan of the Cave Bear
Taken by the Chieftess
Passed Around
Keeping Warm
Her Pretty Pet
Dominated
Seduced
Caught
Savaged

Cyber Mech
Good With Her Hands

Fallen Stars

Fragile Hearts
Broken Minds
Digital Heartbeats
Electric Souls
Metal Bones

Her First Knight
The Knight of the Wild
Sparrow Song
Rowan's Hammer
The Dragon of Almara
Sanctuary
The Flower of Adwean
The Halls of Erinyel
The Daughter of Light
The Tomb of Azmon
Queen Liadan

Knight of Fire
The Queen of Swords
The Three of Goblets
The Queen of Wands
The Queen of Goblets
The Star
The World

Knights of Passion
The Queen's Lust

Handfasting the Warrior Queen
The Revenge of Raven's Cross
The Light of Lythara
Taming the Wolf Knight
The Mermaids of Menosea
The Fairy Queen of Elwenhal
The Dragon of Edhen
Essential Selene
Hearth and Home
Aereth's Return
The Fairy Ring
The Main Course
Knights of Passion: The Complete Series

Knights of Vallor
Saving Salia
Raven Spirit
Eryet's Fountain
The Daughter of Idet
The Mirror of Iovar
Aine's Athenaeum
Bone and Fire
Princess Eydis

Ona of Ozmora
The Amulet of Tizra
The Bandit Queen of Crystal Falls
The Council of Eldor
The Sword of Avara
Wicked Things in the Wilds

Pirates of Artusa
Stolen Booty
Taking Her Sword
Marooned

Tales of the Blood Moon Coven
Bloodlust
The Hidden Memory
Whispered Names
Morbid Fascination
Bending to Her Will
Blood Rage
Prey
Hunted
Voyeuristic Intentions
Interludes and Ecstasy

The Assassin's Kiss
Crossed Daggers
Swordplay

The Chronicles of Omicron
The Thieves of Nottica
The Watchtower of Rustoria

The Dragon Riders of Valheera
Birthday Surprises

The Dreamscape
Out of Mind
Recalling Color

The Last Queen of Qorlec
Project Mothership
The Harvest
The Suns of Anarchy
The Light-year Lion
Moon Fire
Exiled Stars
Zora's Stone

The Legend of Kiva
The Starlight Stair

The Pussycat Chronicles
The Heist
Broken Hearts and Brain Damage
Candy, Sweat, and Regret
Lip Gloss and Loose Women

Witch Xim
Rezzora's Workshop

Standalone
Qorth
Fall Apart World
Unicorn Blood

About the Author

Ash Gray is a lesbian living in California. She writes lesfic (aka fiction for lesbians) in science fiction, fantasy, and paranormal settings.